The
BOX

Illustrated by
Martha Lightfoot

little bee

"What's inside?" asked Annie.

"I don't know," said Flora.
"But whatever it is, can it be mine?"

Annie walked slowly around the empty box.
"I know, **it's a monkey!**"

"Can it still be mine?" said Flora.

Annie ran inside, shouting,

"I'm just going to get some bananas in case it's hungry!"

"Can I have one," called Flora.

When Annie came back, she looked at the box
and said, "Hmmm. The box is too big.
Maybe it's an elephant!"

Flora sat on the swing eating a banana,
thinking the monkey might have liked to swing too.
"Whatever, can it still be mine?" she said.

Annie ran back inside, saying,
"I'm just going to get
a spotted handkerchief
in case he has a runny nose!"

"Can you get me one?" sniffed Flora.

When Annie came back, she stood in front
of the box and said, "Oh. The box is really tall.
Maybe it's a giraffe!"

Flora sat in the long grass, thinking
this was a great place for an elephant.
"Maybe, but can it still be mine?" she said.

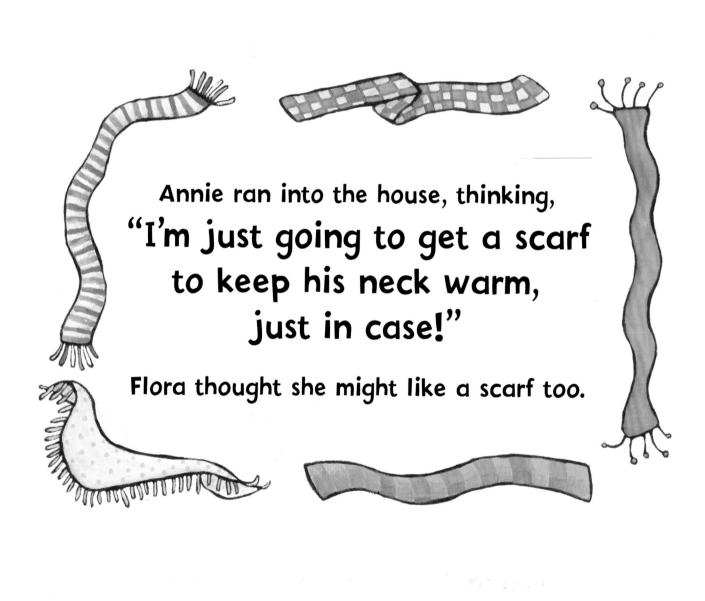

Annie ran into the house, thinking,
"I'm just going to get a scarf
to keep his neck warm,
just in case!"

Flora thought she might like a scarf too.

When Annie came back she saw that
the edge of the box looked a bit chewed.
"Maybe it's a crocodile inside!" she gasped.

Flora thought for a minute.
"In that case, I think it might be yours," she said.

Annie wasn't too sure.
She thought it might need
a toothbrush after its
long journey.

Flora looked up at the treetops and thought the giraffe would have been more fun.

"Dinner time!" came a voice from inside the house.
Annie and Flora looked at the box for a while.

"Let's come back later!" they said and went inside.

"I think they had better
wait outside though,
don't you?!"

For Evie and Nathaniel
M.L.

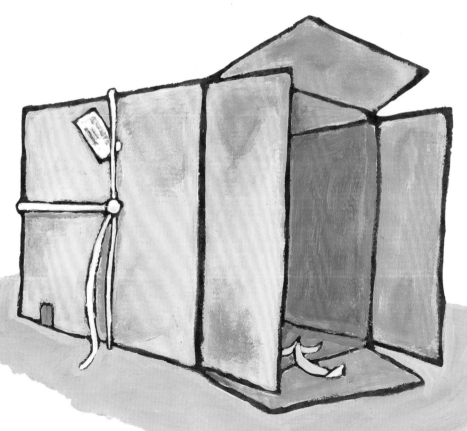

First published in 2006
by Meadowside Children's Books
185 Fleet Street, London EC4A 2HS

This edition published 2009 by Little Bee
an imprint of Meadowside Children's Books

Illustrations © Martha Lightfoot 2006
The right of Martha Lightfoot to be
identified as the illustrator has been
asserted by her in accordance with
the Copyright, Designs and
Patents Act, 1988

A CIP catalogue record for this book
is available from the British Library
10 9 8 7 6 5 4 3 2
Printed in China